LITTLE WOMEN

LITTLE WOMEN

by
Louisa May Alcott

**Abridged, adapted,
and illustrated**
by

quadrum■

Quadrum Solutions, India

Modern Publishing
A Division of Unisystems, Inc.
New York, New York 10022

Series UPC: 38170

Cover art by Marcel Laverdet

Contents

CHAPTER 1

Playing Pilgrims

"Christmas won't be Christmas without any presents," grumbled Jo.

"It's so dreadful to be poor!" said Meg.

"I don't think it's fair for some girls to have plenty of pretty things and other girls to have nothing," added little Amy.

"We've got Father and Mother and each other," Beth said contentedly.

The four young faces brightened at the cheerful words. Jo said sadly, "We haven't got Father, and won't have him for a long time." He was far away, where the war was, and might not ever come home.

They were quiet for a minute. Then Meg said, "You know why Mother said we should not have any presents this Christmas? It's going to be a hard winter."

The four sisters sat knitting in front of the fire. Margaret, or Meg, the eldest, was sixteen years old and very pretty, with large eyes and soft brown hair. Fifteen-year-old Josephine, called Jo, was tall, thin, and

tan, like a colt that didn't know what to do with its long legs. Her long, thick hair was gorgeous. Elizabeth, or Beth, was a rosy, smooth-haired, bright-eyed girl of thirteen, shy, with a timid voice, and a peaceful expression. Amy, the youngest, was twelve. She had blue eyes, and yellow hair curling down to her shoulders; she was pale and slim and walked like a young lady minding her manners.

It was six o'clock. Mother, whom they called Marmee, would soon be there, so everyone's mood got brighter. Jo forgot how tired she was and held her mother's slippers closer to the fire to get warm.

"They are quite worn out. Marmee must have a new pair."

"I'll tell you what . . . let's each of us get her something for Christmas," said Beth.

Everyone thought for a minute, then Meg announced, "I shall give her a nice pair of gloves."

"Army shoes, best to be had," cried Jo.

"Some handkerchiefs, all hemmed," said Beth.

"I'll get a little bottle of cologne. She'll like it," added Amy.

"Glad to find you so happy, girls!" The four sisters turned to welcome a tall, motherly lady. She was not elegantly dressed, but the girls thought she was the most splendid mother in the world.

As they sat at the table, Mrs. March said, smiling, "I've got a treat for you after supper. A nice long letter from Father. He is well. He sends loving wishes for Christmas and a special message to you girls." It was a cheerful letter full of stories about camp life, marches, and military news. Only at the end did he speak of fatherly love and longing for the little girls at home.

"Give them all my dear love and a kiss," the letter said. "Tell them I think of them by day, pray for them by night. A year

seems very long to wait before I see them, but remind them that while we wait we may all work so that these hard days need not be wasted. I know they will remember all I said to them, that they will be loving children to you, will do their duty faithfully, fight their enemies bravely, and conquer themselves so beautifully that when I come back to them I may be fonder and prouder than ever of my little women." Everybody sniffed when they came to that part.

Mrs. March said cheerfully, "Do you remember how you used to play Pilgrim's Progress when you were little? You liked me to tie my bags on your backs for burdens and let you travel through the house from the cellar to the housetop! Look under your pillows on Christmas morning and you will find your guidebook."

They talked over the new plan while old Hannah, the maid servant, cleared the table. The girls started knitting a sheet for Aunt March. At nine they stopped the work and sang, as usual, before they went to bed.

CHAPTER 2

A Merry Christmas

On Christmas day, Jo was the first to wake up. There were no stockings hung at the fireplace and she was really disappointed. She remembered her mother's promise and looked under her pillow. There was a small red-covered book there. She knew what it was—a true guidebook for any pilgrim going on a long journey. She woke Meg up, saying, "Merry Christmas," and told her to see what was under *her* pillow. A green-covered book appeared, with the same picture inside, and a few words written by their mother, which made that present very precious. Soon Beth

and Amy woke up, too, to find their little books, one dove colored, the other blue. The four sisters sat quietly reading from their presents.

At breakfast, the girls sat at the table.

"Merry Christmas, Marmee! Thank you for our books. We read some, and mean to every day," they all cried in chorus.

"Merry Christmas, little daughters! I'm glad you began at once. There is a problem. A poor woman has a little newborn baby. Six children are huddled in one bed, hungry and cold. Will you give them your breakfast as a Christmas present?"

They were all unusually hungry, but they all knew what to do. Jo exclaimed, "I'm so glad you came before we began!"

They were soon ready, and the procession set out. When they got there, they found a poor, miserable room with broken windows, no fire, ragged bedclothes, a sick mother, a wailing baby, and a group of pale, hungry children cuddled under one old quilt, trying to keep warm.

Big eyes stared and blue lips smiled as the girls went in. "*Ach, mein Gott!* It is good angels come to us!" said the poor woman, crying for joy.

It was a very happy breakfast, even though they didn't get any of it. And when they went home, the four little girls were happy with bread and milk for breakfast on Christmas morning and content they had left comfort behind.

When it came to present time, there

was a great deal of love in the small
bundles, and the tall vase of red roses,
white chrysanthemums, and trailing vines
gave quite an elegant air to the table.

Beth played her gayest march on the
piano. Amy threw open the door, and Meg
did her part. Mrs. March was touched and,
with tears of joy in her eyes, she examined
her presents one by one. She put on the

slippers, a new handkerchief was slipped into her pocket, well scented with Amy's cologne, the rose was pinned on her dress, and the gloves fit perfectly.

At supper, they were amazed to see ice cream and cake and fruit and French bonbons and, in the middle of the table, four large bouquets of hothouse flowers.

"Old Mr. Laurence has sent it," said Mrs. March. "Hannah told one of his servants about your breakfast party. He wished to send my children something small for Christmas. I could not refuse."

"That boy put it into his head, I know he did! He looks as if he'd like to know us but he's shy, and Meg won't let me speak to him," said Jo.

"You mean the people who live in the

big house next door, don't you?" asked one of the girls. "Mr. Laurence. He doesn't like to mix with his neighbors. He keeps his grandson in the house, when he isn't riding or walking with his tutor, and makes him study very hard."

CHAPTER 3

The Laurence Boy

"Jo! Jo! Where are you?" cried Meg.

"Here!" answered a husky voice from above. Meg found her sister eating apples.

"Such fun! Here's an invitation from Mrs. Gardiner for tomorrow night!" cried Meg. "Marmee is willing to let us go—now what shall we wear?"

"If I only had a silk!" Meg sighed. "Mother says I may when I'm eighteen, but two years is a long time to wait."

"I'm sure our pops look like silk. Yours is as good as new, but I forgot the burn and the tear in mine."

"I shall have a new ribbon for my hair, and Marmee will lend me her pearl pin."

Meg went away to "accept with thanks" and look over her dress while Jo finished her story.

On New Year's Eve the parlor was deserted, for the two younger girls played dressing maids and the two elder ones were absorbed in "getting ready for the party." Meg wanted a few curls about her face, and Jo undertook to pinch the papered locks with a pair of hot tongs.

"Ought they to smoke like that?" asked Beth from her perch on the bed.

"It's the dampness drying," replied Jo.

"What a queer smell! It's like burned feathers," observed Amy.

"There, now I'll take off the papers and you'll see a cloud of little ringlets," said Jo, putting down the tongs.

She did take off the papers, but no cloud of ringlets appeared, for the hair came with

the papers, and the horrified hairdresser laid a row of little scorched bundles on the bureau before her victim.

"Oh, oh, oh! What have you done? I'm spoiled! I can't go! My hair, oh, my hair!" wailed Meg, looking with despair at the uneven frizzle on her forehead.

"Just my luck! You shouldn't have asked me to do it. I always spoil everything. I'm so sorry; the tongs were too hot, and so I've made a mess," groaned poor Jo.

"It isn't spoiled. Just frizzle it, and tie your ribbon so the ends come on your forehead a bit, and it will look like the latest fashion. I've seen many girls do it so," said Amy consolingly.

"Have a very good time, dearies!" said Mrs. March as the sisters went daintily down the walk. "Don't eat much supper, and come away at eleven when I send Hannah for you."

They seldom went to parties. A stately old lady, Mrs. Gardiner, greeted them kindly and handed them over to the eldest of her six daughters. Meg knew Sallie and was at her ease very soon, but Jo stood with her back carefully against the wall, and felt as much out of place as a colt in a flower garden. She saw a big redheaded youth

walking toward her and, afraid he would ask her to dance, she ran behind the curtain. Unfortunately, another bashful person was already there; she found herself face-to-face with "the Laurence boy."

"Dear me, I didn't know anyone was here!" said Jo, preparing to back out.

But the boy laughed and said, "Don't mind me, stay if you like. How are you, Miss March?" asked the boy.

"Nicely, thank you, Mr. Laurence. But I am not Miss March—I'm only Jo."

"I'm not Mr. Laurence, I'm only Laurie. My first name is Theodore, but I don't like it, for the fellows called me Dora."

"I hate my name, too! I wish everyone would say Jo instead of Josephine."

Both chatted like old friends. Laurie's bashfulness soon wore off, and Jo was her merry self again. She liked "the Laurence boy" better than ever.

CHAPTER 4

Burdens

"Oh, dear, how hard it is to go," sighed Meg the morning after the party as they left to go out.

"Well, don't let us grumble," said Jo.

Everyone seemed rather out of sorts. Saying good-bye, Jo tramped away with Meg. They looked back before turning the corner, for their mother was always at the window to nod and smile, and wave.

When Mr. March lost his property in trying to help a friend, the two oldest girls wanted to help. Margaret found a place as nursery governess and felt rich with her small salary. Jo happened to suit Aunt March, who was lame and needed an active person to wait upon her.

Jo wanted to do something splendid. What it was, she had no idea as yet. Her life was a series of ups and downs. But the training she received at Aunt March's was just what she needed.

Beth was too shy to go to school. She did her lessons at home with her father. Even when he went away, Beth went on by herself and did her best. She loved music so dearly, tried so hard to learn, and practiced so patiently. "I know I'll get my music sometime, if I'm good," she hoped. There are many Beths in the world, shy and quiet, sitting in the corners till needed, and always living for others so cheerfully that no one sees the sacrifices till the little cricket on the hearth stops chirping, and the sweet, sunshiny presence vanishes, leaving silence and shadow behind.

Little Women

Amy's greatest problem was her nose. When she was a baby, Jo had accidentally dropped her, and Amy insisted that it had ruined her nose forever. It was rather flat, and Amy hated it. "Little Raphael," as her sisters called her, had a talent for drawing, and spent time copying flowers, designing fairies, or illustrating stories.

Meg was Amy's confidant and monitor, and by some strange attraction of opposites, Jo was gentle Beth's. To Jo alone did the shy child tell her thoughts, and over her big harum-scarum sister Beth unconsciously exercised more influence than anyone in the family. The two older girls meant a great deal to each other, but each took one of the younger sisters into her keeping and watched over her in her own way, "playing mother," they called it, and put their sisters in the place of discarded dolls with the maternal instinct of little women.

CHAPTER 5

Being Neighborly

"What in the world are you going to do, Jo?" asked Meg.

"Go out for some exercise," answered Jo, a mischievous twinkle in her eyes.

Jo dug paths through the snow with great energy. The garden separated the Marches' house from that of Mr. Laurence. On one side of the hedge was an old, brown shabby house. On the other was a stately stone mansion.

To Jo, it seemed an enchanted palace. She had long wanted to peek inside and to know the Laurence boy. "I think that boy is suffering for society and fun," she said to herself.

Jo saw Mr. Laurence drive off. She then went out to dig her way down to the hedge. It was all quiet. A curly black head leaning on a thin hand looked out of the upper window.

She threw a snowball at him, and the big eyes brightened and the mouth began to smile. Jo nodded and laughed and flourished her broom. "How do you do? Are you sick?"

Laurie opened the window and croaked, "Much better, thank you. I've had a bad cold."

"I'll come, if Mother will let me. I'll go ask her."

Jo marched into the house. Laurie ran around to get ready, brushing his curly hair, and trying to tidy up the room. A servant came to announce a young lady.

"All right, show her up, it's Miss Jo," said Laurie. Jo appeared, with a covered dish in one hand and Beth's three kittens in the other.

"Here I am, bag and baggage," she said. "Mother sent her love. Meg wanted me to bring some of her blancmange, and Beth thought her cats would be comforting."

"Is Beth the rosy one, who stays at home a good deal and sometimes goes out with a little basket?" asked Laurie.

"Yes, that's Beth. She's my girl, and a regular good one she is, too."

"The pretty one is Meg, and the curly-haired one is Amy, I believe? I often hear you calling to one another."

"Well, I just wish you'd come over and see us. Wouldn't your grandpa let you?"

"You see, Grandpa lives among his books. Mr. Brooke, my tutor, doesn't stay here, you know, and I have no one to go out with me."

Laurie led Jo to the library, where she clapped her hands and pranced, as she always did when she was happy. It was lined with books, and there were pictures, statues, and cabinets full of coins and curiosities.

The doctor came, and Laurie went away. Jo was standing before a fine portrait of the old gentleman when the door opened again and, without turning, she said, "I'm sure now that I shouldn't be afraid of him, for he's got kind eyes."

"Thank you, ma'am," said a gruff voice belonging to Mr. Laurence. Jo blushed. She saw that the eyes under the bushy eyebrows were kind, with a sly twinkle in them. The gruff voice was gruffer, as the old gentleman said, "So you're not afraid of me, hey?"

"Not much, sir."

"What have you been doing to this boy of mine, hey?" was the next question, sharply put.

"Only trying to be neighborly, sir." And

Jo told how her visit came about.

"You think he needs cheering up?"

"Yes, sir, he seems a little lonely, and young folks would do him good perhaps."

The tea bell rang. Laurie came back.

The old gentleman did not say much as he drank his tea, but he watched the young people, chatting away like old friends, and the change in his grandson did not escape him. There was color, light, and life in the boy's face now.

She's right. The lad is lonely. I'll see what these little girls can do for him, thought Mr. Laurence as he looked and listened. He liked Jo.

Laurie played the piano, and Jo listened. Mr. Laurence said, "His music isn't bad, but I hope he will do as well in more important things. Going? I hope you'll come again. My respects to your mother. Good night, Doctor Jo."

Back at home, when all the afternoon's adventures had been told, the family wanted to go visiting. Mrs. March wanted to talk of her father with the old man who had not forgotten him, Meg longed to walk in the conservatory, Beth sighed for the grand piano, and Amy was eager to see the fine pictures and statues.

"Laurie's a nice boy and I like him. We'll all be good to him because he hasn't got any mother, and he may come over and see us, mayn't he, Marmee?" Jo said, very eager.

"Yes, Jo, your friend is very welcome."

CHAPTER 6

Beth Finds
the Palace Beautiful

The big house did prove a Palace Beautiful, though it took some time for all to get in. Beth found it very hard to pass the lions. Old Mr. Laurence was the biggest one, but after he had said something funny or kind to each of the girls and talked with their mother, nobody felt much afraid of him, except timid Beth.

Meg could walk in the conservatory whenever she liked, Jo browsed the books in the new library, Amy copied pictures and enjoyed beauty, and Laurie played "lord of the manor."

But Beth, though longing for the grand piano, was not brave enough to go to the big house. She went once with Jo, but the old gentleman stared and said "Hey!" so loud that he frightened her, and she ran away.

Mr. Laurence heard about it and when he called one day, as if the idea had just occurred to him, he said to Mrs. March, "The boy neglects his music now. And the piano suffers for want of use. Wouldn't some of your girls like to run over and practice on it, just to keep it in tune? Please, tell the young ladies what I say, and if they don't care to come, why, never mind." Here a little hand slipped into his, and Beth looked up at him with a face full of gratitude.

"Oh, sir. They do care to come, very much! I'm Beth. I'd love it dearly, and I'll come, if you are quite sure nobody will be disturbed."

"Not a soul, my dear."

Beth blushed like a rose and gave the hand a grateful squeeze. Next day, Beth made her way noiselessly to the drawing room. Quite by accident, of course, some pretty, easy music lay on the piano. Beth at last touched the great instrument and forgot her fear, herself, and everything else but the delight that the music gave her.

She stayed till Hannah came to take her home; she had no appetite for food and could only sit and smile at everyone.

After that, the great drawing room was haunted by a tuneful spirit that went unseen. She never knew that Mr. Laurence left his study door open to hear the music. She never saw Laurie guarding the hall to warn the servants away. She never knew that the exercise books and new song books in the rack were put there for her.

"Oh, Mother, I'm going to work a pair

of slippers for Mr. Laurence. He is so kind to me, I must thank him. Can I do it?" asked Beth a few weeks later.

"Yes, dear. It will please him very much," replied Mrs. March.

The pattern was chosen, the materials bought, and the slippers begun. Beth worked hard on them. Then she wrote a short, simple note and, with Laurie's help, got them smuggled onto the study table one

morning before the old gentleman was up.

On the afternoon of the second day, she went out. As she came back home, several joyful voices screamed, "Here's a letter from the kind, old gentleman! Come quick, and read it!"

At the door her sisters pulled her to the parlor, all pointing and saying at once, "Look there!" There stood a little cabinet piano, with a letter lying on the glossy lid, directed to "Miss Elizabeth March."

"Miss March—'Dear Madam, I have had many pairs of slippers in my life, but I never had any that suited me so well as yours,' " read Jo. "I know you will allow 'the old gentleman' to send you something that once belonged to the little grand-daughter he lost. With hearty thanks and best wishes, I remain your grateful friend and humble servant, JAMES LAURENCE."

"Try it, honey. Let's hear the sound of the baby pianny," said Hannah. So Beth

tried it, and everyone said it was the best piano music ever heard.

"You'll have to go and thank him," said Jo.

"Yes, I mean to." And, to everyone's amazement, Beth walked down the garden to the Laurences' door.

She knocked at the study door. When a gruff voice called out, "Come in!" she did go in, right up to Mr. Laurence. She held out her hand. "I came to thank you, sir, for . . ." But she didn't finish, for he looked so friendly that she forgot her speech, and she put both arms around his neck and kissed him.

CHAPTER 7

Secrets

Jo was very busy in the garret, seated on the old sofa, writing busily. Scrabble, the pet rat, walked along the beams overhead, accompanied by his oldest son. Jo scribbled away till the last page was filled. Then she signed her name with a flourish and threw down her pen, exclaiming, "There, I've done my best!"

She read the manuscript carefully, making dashes here and there, and putting in many exclamation points. Then she tied it up with a smart red ribbon and sat a minute looking at it with a sober, wistful expression. From her desk Jo produced another manuscript and, putting both in her pocket, crept quietly downstairs.

She put on her hat and jacket quietly and sneaked out of the house. Jumping into a bus, she went to town. There, she got off the bus and did something strange. She walked fast to a certain number in a certain

busy street. Having found the place, she went into the doorway, looked up the dirty stairs and, after standing still for a minute, suddenly walked away as fast as she came. This she did several times, and the black-eyed young gentleman in the window of a building opposite smiled. The third time, Jo gave herself a shake, pulled her hat over her eyes, and walked up the stairs.

There was a dentist's sign, among others, at the entrance, and after staring at it for a minute, the young gentleman put on his coat, took his hat, and went down to stand in the opposite doorway, saying, "If she has a bad time, she'll need someone to help her get home."

In ten minutes Jo came running downstairs with a very red face.

"Did you have a bad time?"

he asked.

"Not very."

"How many did you have out?"

Jo looked at her friend and then laughed. "There are two that I want to have out, but I must wait a week. Well, I've left two stories with a newspaperman, and he's to give his answer next week," whispered Jo.

"Hurrah for Miss March, the celebrated American authoress!" cried Laurie.

Jo's eyes sparkled.

For a week or two, Jo behaved strangely. She rushed to the door when the postman rang, was rude to Mr. Brooke, would sit looking at Meg sadly, then jump up to shake and then kiss her. On the second Saturday after Jo's trip, Meg saw Laurie chasing Jo all over the garden and finally capturing her in Amy's bower. Shrieks of laughter were heard, followed by voices and a great flapping of newspapers.

In a few minutes Jo bounced in, lay down on the sofa, and pretended to read.

"Is there anything interesting to read?" asked Meg.

"Nothing but a story," said Jo.

"'The Rival Painters,'" Jo said, and began to read fast. The story was romantic,

and somewhat sad, as most of the characters died in the end.

"Who wrote it?" asked Beth.

The reader suddenly sat up, pushed aside the paper, and said, "Your sister."

Meg wouldn't believe it till she saw the words "Miss Josephine March" actually printed in the paper. Amy offered hints for a sequel that couldn't happen. Beth got excited and skipped and sang with joy. Hannah came in to join in. How proud Mrs. March was when she found out about it!

CHAPTER 8

A Telegram

"November is the most disagreeable month in the whole year," said Margaret, standing at the window one dull afternoon, looking out at the frostbitten garden.

"That's the reason I was born in it," observed Jo pensively.

"If something very pleasant should happen now, we should think it a delightful month," said Beth.

"I dare say but nothing pleasant ever does happen in this family," said Meg. Hannah came in with a letter. "It's a telegram, Mum," she said.

Mrs. March snatched it, read the two lines it contained, and dropped back into her chair. Her face was white. Laurie dashed downstairs for water while Meg and Hannah held Mrs. March and Jo read aloud, in a frightened voice:

"'Mrs. March:
Your husband is very ill. Please come at once.
S. HALE, Blank Hospital,
Washington.'"

Mrs. March read the message over and stretched out her arms to her daughters, saying, "I shall go at once, but it may be too late. Laurie, send a telegram saying I will come at once. The next train goes early in the morning. I'll take that. Leave a note at Aunt March's."

She wrote a note. "Now go, dear, but don't kill yourself driving too fast." The happy household was broken up. Mr. Laurence came hurrying back with

Beth. Mr. Brooke said, "I'm very sorry to hear of this, Miss March. I came to offer myself as an escort to your mother."

"How kind you all are! Mother will accept, I'm sure. Thank you very, very much!" Meg led the way into the parlor,

saying she would call her mother.

Everything was ready and all errands were done, but Jo had vanished. They began to get anxious. But she came in soon after, with a strange look on her face, a mixture of fun and fear, satisfaction and regret. She gave her mother a wad of money, saying, "That's my contribution!"

"My dear, where did you get it? Twenty-five dollars!"

"No, it's mine, honestly. I only sold what was my own."

As she spoke, Jo took off her bonnet. Her hair was short.

"Your hair! Your beautiful hair!"

"Oh, Jo, how could you do that? Your one beauty."

"My dear girl, there was no need of doing this."

"She doesn't look like my Jo anymore, but I love her dearly for it!"

Everyone was surprised. "Tell me all

about it, Jo," said Mrs. March.

"Well, I was wild to do something for Father," replied Jo. "I didn't think of selling my hair at first, but then in a barber's window I saw hair with the prices marked, and one, not so thick as mine, was forty dollars. I walked in, asked if they bought hair, and what they would give for mine.

The man said mine was not a fashionable color, and he never paid much for it. I begged him to take it, and told him why I was in such a hurry. I took a last look at my hair while the man got his things, and that was the end of it."

"Go to bed and don't talk, for we must be up early and shall need all the sleep we can get. Good night, my darlings," said Mrs. March.

They kissed her quietly and went to bed. Beth and Amy soon fell asleep, but Meg lay awake, thinking the most serious thoughts. Jo lay still and then sobbed.

"Jo, dear, what is it? Are you crying about father?"

"No—My . . . my hair!" burst out poor Jo.

CHAPTER 9

Letters

In the cold, gray dawn the sisters lit their lamp and read their chapters with an earnestness never felt before. For now the shadow of a real trouble had come, the little books were full of help and comfort, and as they dressed, they agreed to say good-bye cheerfully and hopefully and send their mother on her journey unsaddened by tears or complaints from them.

Everything seemed very strange when the girls went down; it was dim and still outside, but full of light and bustle within.

Nobody talked much, but as the time for her to leave drew near, Mrs. March said to the girls, "Children, I leave you to Hannah's care and Mr. Laurence's protection. Go on with your work as usual. Hope and keep busy, and whatever happens, remember that you never can be fatherless."

"We will, Mother! We will!"

The carriage arrived. No one cried; they all sent loving messages to Father. They kissed their mother, hugged her, and waved cheerfully when she drove away.

As she rolled away, the sun came out; Mrs. March saw it shining on the group at the gate like a good omen. They smiled and waved, and the last thing she saw was four bright faces, and behind them like bodyguards, old Mr. Laurence, faithful Hannah, and devoted Laurie.

"I feel as if there had been an earthquake," said Jo at home.

"It seems as if half the house was gone,"

added Meg.

Beth pointed to the pile of nicely mended stockings on the table, showing that even in her last hurried moments Marmee had thought and worked for them. They all broke down and cried bitterly.

Hannah wisely allowed them to relieve their feelings, and then came with a

coffeepot.

"Now, my dear young ladies, remember what your ma said, and don't fret. Come and have a cup of coffee all around, and then let's fall to work and be a credit to the family."

News from their father comforted the girls very much, for though he was very ill, his wife's being there had already done him good. Mr. Brooke sent a letter every day. And the girls wrote back.

CHAPTER 10

Little Faithful

For a week, everyone was very good. Once they heard that their father was better, things were more relaxed. Jo caught a bad cold because she forgot to cover her shorn head and had to stay at home until she got better.

Amy went back to her clay sculpting. Meg did her work, but spent a lot of time reading letters from Washington or writing long letters to her mother. Beth kept on going, without showing her sadness.

"Meg, I wish you'd go and see the Hummels. You know Mother told us not to forget them," Beth said, ten days after Mrs. March had left.

"I'm too tired to go this afternoon," replied Meg.

"Can't you, Jo?" asked Beth.

"Too stormy for me with my cold."

So Beth lay down on the sofa, and the Hummels were forgotten. An hour passed. Amy did not come, Meg went to her room to try on a new dress, Jo was absorbed in her story, and Hannah was sound asleep before the kitchen fire when Beth quietly put on her hood, filled her basket with odds and ends for the poor children, and went out into the chilly air with a heavy heart and a grieved look in her patient eyes.

It was late when she came back, and no one saw her creep upstairs and shut herself into her mother's room. Half an hour later, Jo found little Beth sitting on the bed, looking very serious, with red eyes and a camphor bottle in her hand.

"What's the matter?" cried Jo. "You've had scarlet fever, haven't you?"

"Oh, Jo, the baby's dead!"

"What baby?"

"Mrs. Hummel's. It died in my lap before she got home," Beth sobbed.

"Now I'll tell you what we'll do," said Hannah, when she had examined and questioned Beth. "We will have Dr. Bangs over, just to take a look at you, dear, and see that we start right. Then we'll send Amy off to Aunt March's for a spell, to keep her out of harm's way."

Dr. Bangs came, and said that Beth had symptoms of the fever, but he thought that she would have it lightly. In the meantime, Amy departed, with Jo and Laurie as an escort.

CHAPTER 11

Dark Days

Beth did have the fever, and was much sicker than anyone but Hannah and the doctor suspected. Meg stayed at home and kept house, feeling guilty when she wrote letters to her mother, never talking about Beth's illness.

Jo was with Beth day and night. At some stage, the little girl began to talk in a hoarse, broken voice and called for her mother. Jo grew frightened, Meg wanted to write the truth to Marmee, but Hannah said there was no danger yet. Mr. March had a relapse, and could not think of coming home for a long while. Beth was very ill, going in and out of consciousness.

The first of December was a wintry day. When Dr. Bangs came that morning, he examined Beth, held her hot hand in both of his own for a minute, and said to Hannah, "If Mrs. March can leave her husband, she should come."

Jo ran to the parlor, snatched up the telegram, and rushed out into the storm. She was soon back, and Laurie came in with a letter saying that Mr. March was getting better again. Jo read it thankfully, but looked so upset that Laurie asked, "Is Beth worse?"

"Yes, she is. She doesn't look like my Beth, and there's nobody to help us bear it. Mother and father are both gone, and God seems so far away, I can't find Him."

As the tears streamed fast down poor Jo's cheeks, she stretched out her hand in a helpless sort of way, as if groping in the

dark, and Laurie took it in his, whispering as well as he could with a lump in his throat, "I'm here. Hold on to me, Jo, dear!"

She could not speak, but she did "hold on," and the warm grasp of the friendly human hand comforted her. Laurie longed to say something tender and comfortable, but no fitting words came to him, so he stood silent, gently stroking Jo's bent head as her mother used to do.

It was the best thing he could have done, for Jo felt the unspoken sympathy. Soon she dried the tears that had relieved her, and looked up with a grateful face.

"Thank you, Teddy, I'm better now."

"Keep hoping for the best, Jo. Soon your mother will be here, and then everything will be all right."

A breath of fresh air seemed to blow through the house and something brightened the quiet rooms. Everyone rejoiced but Beth. She lay unconscious of anything.

It was past two when Jo heard a movement by the bed and, turning quickly, saw Meg kneeling in front of their mother's chair with her face hidden. A dreadful fear came to Jo. "Beth is dead, and Meg is afraid to tell me."

She looked at Beth. The fever flush and the look of pain were gone, and the little face looked so pale and peaceful

that Jo couldn't cry. Leaning low over her sister, she kissed the damp forehead and softly whispered, "Good-bye, my Beth. Good-bye!"

Hannah woke up, hurried to the bed, looked at Beth, felt her hands, and then exclaimed, "The fever's turned, she's sleepin' nat'ral, her skin's damp, and she breathes easy. Praise be given! Oh, my goodness me!"

The doctor arrived just then and confirmed it. He smiled and said, "Yes, my dears, I think the little girl will pull through this time. Keep the house quiet, let her sleep."

"If Mother would only come now!" said Jo.

There was a sound of bells at the door below, a cry from Hannah, and then Laurie's voice saying in a joyful whisper, "Girls, she's come! She's come!"

CHAPTER 12

Amy's Hard Times

Amy was having hard times at Aunt March's, who meant to be kind, for the well-behaved little girl pleased her very much. Amy liked the Indian cabinet, full of queer drawers, little pigeonholes, and secret places, storing all sorts of trinkets, some precious, some not, all old.

I like the diamonds best. But I should choose this if I might, thought Amy, looking at a string of gold and ebony beads with a heavy cross. "I wish I knew where all these pretty things would go when Aunt March dies," she told Esther, the maid.

"I think that the little turquoise ring will be given to you when you go, for Madame approves of you."

Esther set up a small prayer chapel for Amy, with a table, a footstool, and a picture of the Divine Mother. On the table she put her little testament and hymnbook, kept a vase of the best flowers Laurie brought her, and came every day to "sit alone" thinking good thoughts and praying for her sister.

CHAPTER 13

Confidential

When Beth awoke, the first things she saw were the little rose and Mother's face. Then she slept again.

Meg and Jo fed their mother while they listened to her whispered account of Father's health, Mr. Brooke's promise to stay and nurse him, the journey home, and Laurie waiting for her at the station.

The house was still. Mrs. March would not leave Beth's side, but rested in the big chair. Laurie drove off to see Amy, and both the little girl and Aunt March were relieved and happy. Mrs. March also came to visit.

Amy and her mother sat alone together in the chapel for a while.

"I like it very much, dear," said Marmee. "It is an excellent plan to have someplace where we can go to be quiet when we are upset."

As Amy pointed to the picture, Mrs. March saw the ring on her hand and smiled. Amy said, "Aunt gave me the ring today. I'd like to wear it, Mother."

"It is very pretty, but I think you're rather too young, Amy," said Mrs. March.

That evening Jo went to Beth's room.

"What is it, dear?" asked Mrs. March.

"Last summer Meg left a pair of gloves over at the Laurences' and only one was returned. We forgot about it till Teddy told me that Mr. Brooke had owned up that he liked Meg but didn't dare say so, she was so young and he so poor."

"Do you think Meg cares for him?" asked Mrs. March.

"Mercy me! I don't know anything about love and such nonsense!" cried Jo.

"My dear, don't get angry about it. John went with me, at Mr. Laurence's request, and was so devoted to poor Father that we couldn't help becoming fond of him. He was perfectly open and honorable about Meg, for he told us he loved her but would earn a comfortable home before he asked her to marry him."

CHAPTER 14

Pleasant Meadows

Like the sunshine after a storm, the weeks that followed were peaceful and happy. Mr. March began to talk of returning early in the new year. Beth was soon able to lie on the study sofa all day and, in time, with doll's sewing. Meg learned how to cook, while Amy started giving away many of her treasures.

As Christmas approached, Jo and Laurie came up with all sorts of impossible ideas to celebrate. Mr. March wrote that he should soon be home. Then Beth felt very well as Jo carried her to the window to see the surprise they had made. Out in the garden stood a stately snow maiden, crowned with holly, carrying a basket of fruit and flowers in one hand, a great roll of music in the other, a blanket around her shoulders, and a Christmas carol that came from her lips on a pink paper streamer:

Little Women

THE JUNGFRAU TO BETH
God bless you, dear Queen Bess!
May nothing you dismay,
But health and peace and happiness
Be yours, this Christmas day.

How Beth laughed when she saw it. Now and then, in this busy world, things do happen in a delightful storybook fashion, and what a comfort it is. Laurie opened the door and popped his head in very quietly. He only said, "Here's another Christmas present for the March family."

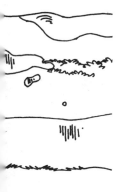

There in the doorway appeared a tall man, leaning on the arm of another tall man. For several minutes everybody seemed to lose their wits, for the strangest things were done, and no one said a word.

Mr. March was invisible

behind four pairs of loving arms. Jo nearly fainted, and had to be doctored by Laurie. Mr. Brooke kissed Meg entirely by mistake. And Amy, the dignified, tripped over a stool, and hugged and cried over her father's boots. Mrs. March was the first to recover, and held up her hand with a warning, "Hush! Remember Beth."

Never mind what happened just after that, for the full hearts overflowed,washing away the bitterness of the past and leaving only the sweetness of the present.

There never was such a Christmas dinner as they had that day. The fat turkey was stuffed, browned, and decorated and looked delicious! So did the plum pudding, which melted in one's mouth. Everything turned out well, which was a mercy.

Mr. Laurence and his grandson dined with them, and also Mr. Brooke. Two easy chairs stood side by side at the head of the table, in which sat Beth and her father,

feasting modestly on chicken and a little fruit. They drank to everyone's health, told stories, sang songs, "reminisced," as the old folks say, and had a thoroughly good time.

CHAPTER 15

Aunt March Settles the Question

Mr. March sat near Beth's sofa, and everyone kept coming into the room to check on them. Meg was absent-minded, shy, and silent, started when the bell rang, and colored when John Brooke's name was mentioned.

There was a step in the hall. Jo laughed to herself and, when someone tapped on the door, opened it.

"Good afternoon. I came to get my umbrella, that is, to see how your father finds himself today," said Mr. Brooke, looking from one face to the other.

"He's very well. I'll get him and tell him you are here." And Jo slipped out of the room. Meg went toward the door, murmuring, "Mother will like to see you. I'll call her."

"Don't go. Are you afraid of me, Meg?" Mr. Brooke asked, and looked hurt.

"How can I be afraid, when you have been so kind to Father? I only wish I could thank you for it."

"Shall I tell you how to be thankful?" asked Mr. Brooke, holding Meg's small hand fast in both his own, looking at her with love in his brown eyes.

"Oh no, please don't, I'd rather you not," she said.

"I won't trouble you. I only want to know if you care for me a little, Meg. I love you so much, dear," added Mr. Brooke.

Meg answered softly, "I don't know."

Little Women

John just stood looking at her so wistfully, so tenderly that she found her heart melting. Just then, Aunt March came hobbling in. Mr. Brooke vanished into the study.

"Bless me, what's all this?" cried the old lady.

"It's Father's friend. I'm so surprised to see you!" stammered Meg.

"Brooke? That boy's tutor? I know all about it. You haven't gone and accepted him, child?" cried Aunt March.

"I shall marry whom I please, Aunt March," Meg said. "I couldn't do better if I waited half my life! John is good and wise, he's got heaps of talent, he's willing to work, and he's so energetic and brave. Everyone likes and respects him, and I'm proud to think he cares for me though I'm so poor and young and silly," said Meg.

Aunt March drove off. Meg stood for a moment, not sure whether to laugh or cry. Before she could make up her mind, she was grabbed by Mr. Brooke, who said, "I couldn't help hearing, Meg. Thank you for defending me. And I needn't go away, but may stay and be happy, may I, dear?"

Meg meekly whispered, "Yes, John," and hid her face.

Fifteen minutes later, when Jo came downstairs, she found Mr. Brooke sitting on the sofa, with Meg on his knee. Jo gasped. Meg jumped up, looking both proud and shy, but John laughed and said, "Sister Jo, congratulate us!"

Rushing upstairs, Jo burst into the room, and said, "Oh, go down quick! John Brooke is acting dreadfully, and Meg likes it!"

Nobody ever knew what went on in the parlor that afternoon. Quiet Mr. Brooke astonished his friends by the way in which he spoke of the future. And he got his way. Everyone was happy, especially Meg and her John.

CHAPTER 16

The First Wedding

Three years passed. The war was now over, and Mr. March was home. Mrs. March was still brisk and cheery, though older, and absorbed in Meg's affairs. John Brooke went to war for a year, got wounded, was sent home, and not allowed to return. He worked on getting well, preparing for business, and earning a home for Meg.

Meg had been working and learning how to be a wife and manage a home, and was becoming prettier than ever. Aunt March liked Amy and offered to pay for drawing lessons for her, so Amy went to her house every day. Jo worked on her writing and looked after Beth, who was not as healthy as she earlier was, but was still hopeful and serene. Laurie went to college to please his grandfather, but was now doing nothing.

The Dovecote was the little brown house Mr. Brooke had found for Meg. It had a little garden behind it and a miniature lawn in the front. Inside, it was charming. The hall was very narrow, the dining room was so small that six people could barely fit in it, and the kitchen stairs were too steep. But there was good sense and good taste, simple furniture, lots of books, nice pictures, flowers, and pretty gifts.

"Are you satisfied? Does it seem like home, and do you feel as if you should be happy here?" asked Mrs. March.

"Yes Mother, very satisfied, thanks to you all. I'm so happy, I can't talk about it."

The June roses over the porch were awake bright and early. On the day of Meg's

wedding, the sisters dressed the bride. She had made her wedding gown herself. Her sisters braided her hair, and the only jewels she wore were lilies of the valley, which "her John" liked best of all.

In three years Jo had learned to carry herself with ease, if not grace. The curly crop had become a thick coil. There was a fresh color in her brown cheeks, a soft shine in her eyes, and she spoke only gentle words today. Beth had grown slender, pale, and more quiet than ever. The beautiful, kind eyes were larger, and held a shadow of pain. Beth seldom complained and always spoke hopefully of "being better soon." Amy was truly "the flower of the family." At sixteen she had the air and bearing of a full-grown woman, not beautiful, but very graceful.

There were to be no ceremonious performances, everything was to be as natural and homelike as possible, so when Aunt March arrived, she was scandalized to see the bride come running to welcome and lead her in, to find the bridegroom fastening up a garland that had fallen down, and to catch a glimpse of the minister marching

upstairs looking serious, with a wine bottle under each arm.

There was no bridal procession, but a sudden silence fell as Mr. March and the young couple took their places under the green arch. Mother and sisters gathered close. Their father's voice broke more than once, which only seemed to make the service more beautiful and solemn. The bridegroom's hand trembled visibly, and no one heard his replies. But Meg looked straight up in her husband's eyes and said, "I will!" with such trust in her own face and voice that her mother's heart rejoiced.

Jo did not cry, though she was very near it once, but Laurie was staring fixedly at her. Beth kept her face hidden on her mother's shoulder, but Amy stood like a graceful statue, with a ray of sunshine touching her white forehead and the flower in her hair.

The minute she was married, Meg cried, "The first kiss for Marmee!" During the next fifteen minutes she looked more like a rose than ever, for everyone kissed her, from

Mr. Laurence to old Hannah. Everybody smiled after that, and said something brilliant, or tried to.

The toast was drunk with lemonade. After lunch, people strolled about

through the house and garden, enjoying the sunshine. Meg and John were standing on the lawn, when Laurie got inspired. "All the married people hold hands and dance around the new-made husband and wife, as the Germans do, while we bachelors and spinsters dance in couples outside!" cried Laurie. Mr. and Mrs. March, Aunt and Uncle Carrol began, others rapidly joined in, even Mr. Laurence and Aunt March.

CHAPTER 17

Artistic Attempts

It takes people time to learn the difference between talent and genius, especially ambitious young men and women. Amy was learning this distinction through much tribulation, for in mistaking enthusiasm for inspiration, she attempted every branch of art with youthful audacity. For a while, she tried pen-and-ink drawing, which she was very good at. Then she tried poker sketching and had the whole family wondering if they would wake up with the house on fire. Then she chose oil painting. Charcoal portraits came next. Softened into crayon sketches, they did better. Then she went back to clay and plaster.

Then Amy started sketching from nature. She caught colds sitting on damp grass. She got tan floating on the river in the sun to study light and shade, and got a wrinkle over her nose trying to get the perspective right.

"My lady," as her friends called her, really wanted to be a genuine lady. She was one, naturally, but had yet to learn that money cannot buy breeding.

"I want to ask a favor of you, Mamma," Amy said one day. "Our drawing class breaks up next week, and before the girls separate for the summer, I want to ask them out here for a day."

"That looks okay. What do you want to have for lunch? Cake, sandwiches, fruit, and coffee?"

"Oh, no! We must have cold tongue and chicken, French chocolate, and ice cream. The girls are used to such things, and I want my lunch to be more proper and elegant."

Mrs. March knew that experience was an excellent teacher. "Very well, Amy, if your heart is set upon it, I'll say no more."

The invitations were sent, nearly all the girls accepted, and the following Monday was chosen for the grand event. Having made up her mind what to do, Amy went about doing it, no matter what.

On Monday morning it drizzled a little, shone a little, blew a little, and the weather was in an undecided state, which was exasperating! Amy was up at dawn, rushing about and waking everyone up. The lunch looked good. Everyone seemed ready to play their part.

Then she waited. At eleven it rained, and at twelve, none of the girls had come. At two, the exhausted family sat down to eat. The next day, only one girl Miss Eliot, arrived. Amy was quite calm and cordial to the guest who had kept her promise. The rest of the family played their parts equally well, and Miss Eliott had fun. The lunch was eaten, the studio and garden visited, and art was discussed with enthusiasm. Amy ordered a buggy and drove her friend about the neighborhood till sunset.

After her friend had left, Amy came back to the house. Everything had been cleared up.

"I'm very sorry you were disappointed, dear, but we all did our best to satisfy you," said Mrs. March.

"I am satisfied. I've done what I undertook, and it's not my fault that it failed," said Amy. "I thank you all very much for helping me, and I'll thank you still more if you won't mention it for a month, at least."

CHAPTER 18

Literary Lessons

Fortune suddenly smiled upon Jo. She had just recovered from a bout of writing when she went for a lecture on the Pyramids. On her right sat a boy reading from a newspaper.

It was a set of pictures, a melodramatic illustration of an Indian in full war costume, tumbling over a cliff with a wolf at his throat, while two angry young gentlemen with very small feet and big eyes were stabbing each other close by, and a woman was flying away in the background with her mouth wide open. The boy saw her looking and offered her half his paper, saying, "Want to read it?"

Jo accepted with a smile, and soon got involved in a story of love, mystery, and murder. "Prime, isn't it?" asked the boy.

"I think you and I could do as well as that if we tried," returned Jo.

"I should think I was a pretty lucky chap if I could. She makes a good living out of such stories, they say."

Jo took down the address of the paper, having decided to try for the hundred-dollar prize offered for a sensational story. By the time the lecture had ended and the audience awoke, she was already deep in her new story, unable to decide whether the duel should come before the elopement or after the murder.

She started work the next day. Her story was full of desperation, set in Lisbon, and ended with an earthquake. The manuscript was sent off.

Six weeks later, when she had almost given up hope, a letter arrived. She opened it; a check for a hundred dollars fell into her lap. She appeared at the table, with the letter in one hand, the check in the other, announcing that she had won the prize. Everyone was thrilled and praised the story. Her father told her that though the

language was good, the romance fresh and hearty, and the tragedy quite thrilling, he also shook his head and said, "You can do better than this, Jo. Aim at the highest, and never mind the money."

Jo started working on more stories. "The Duke's Daughter" paid the butcher's bill, "A Phantom Hand" got them a new carpet, and "The Curse of the Coventrys" bought the family groceries and gowns.

CHAPTER 19

Domestic Experiences

Like most other young wives, Meg began her married life determined to be a model housekeeper. And then she made jam. She did her best, but the stuff wouldn't "jell." At five o'clock in the evening she sat down in her messy kitchen and cried.

John came home then, with a friend. The kitchen was a huge mess. There was jelly dripping everywhere, and the smell of burned sugar was like a cloud over the whole house. And Meg sat there, sobbing.

"The . . . the jelly won't jell, and I don't know what to do!"

John Brooke laughed.

The next summer, Meg was expecting a baby. One happy day, Meg was about to give birth and Laurie came sneaking into the kitchen. Sometime later, Jo appeared, proudly bearing a flannel bundle held on a large pillow. Her face was very sober, but her eyes twinkled. "Shut your eyes and hold out your arms," she said.

"I will! But don't blame me if something happens." Laurie shut his eyes while something was put into his arms. Everyone laughed, including John, as he looked at two babies on his lap instead of one.

"Boy and girl. Aren't they beauties?" said the proud papa.

"Amy put a blue ribbon on the boy and a pink on the girl, so you can always tell. Besides, one has blue eyes and one brown," said Jo.

"The boy's to be named John Laurence, and the girl Margaret, after mother and

grandmother. We shall call them Daisy and Jack, unless we find better names," said Amy.

"Name him Demijohn, and call him Demi for short," said Laurie.

"Daisy and Demi—just the thing! I knew Teddy would do it," cried Jo.

CHAPTER 20

Calls

"Come, Jo, it's time. You promised to make half a dozen calls with me today. "Now put on all your best things, and I'll tell you how to behave at each place."

While Amy dressed, she issued her orders. "The Chesters consider themselves very elegant people, so I want you to put on your best manners that are safe and more ladylike."

Naughty Jo took her literally; during the first call she sat gracefully. Anything anyone said was answered by a smile, a bow, and a "yes" or a "no."

113

Amy was annoyed. "Try to be sociable at the Lambs'. Gossip as other girls do, and be interested in dress and flirtations."

Amy saw her sister skim into the next drawing room, kiss all the young ladies with effusion, beam graciously upon the young gentlemen, and join in the chat with a spirit that amazed the beholder.

"Didn't I do well?" asked Jo.

"Nothing could have been worse," was Amy's crushing reply.

After that, they went to visit Aunt March, but Jo was not in a good mood.

"Are you going to help with the fair, dear?" asked Mrs. Carrol.

Amy replied, "Yes, Aunt."

"It's a pleasure to help people who appreciate our efforts," said Aunt March.

If Jo had only known what the future held, she would have kept quiet. She said, "I don't like favors. I'd rather do everything for myself, and be perfectly independent."

They soon left the place. And Aunt March said, "You'd better do it, Mary. I'll supply the money."

Aunt Carrol replied, "I certainly will, if her father and mother consent."

CHAPTER 21

Consequences

Mrs. Chester's fair was very elegant and select. Amy was asked to handle a table, one that sold art. But May Chester was jealous of Amy. And just when everything was ready, Mrs. Chester said, "I find, dear, that people don't like the idea of my giving this table to anyone but my girls. I'm sorry, but I know you won't mind taking another table."

Amy said, with hurt feelings, "Perhaps you had rather I took no table at all?"

"I think the flower table is always attractive and you would prefer it."

Everyone was annoyed at home that evening when Amy told her story. The next day was a long and hard one for her. She got home late, and looked so pale and quiet that everyone knew the day had been hard. The next morning, she left early.

Jo met Laurie by the gate, and they chatted. Thanks to the conspirators, the tables were turned. Fresh, beautiful flowers came from Mr. Laurence's gardens. And the March family was all there. Laurie and his friends bought the bouquets, stood around the table, and made that corner the liveliest spot in the room. Amy was in her element now.

"Everything of Amy's sold long ago. And they made a nice little sum of money for us," said May.

Aunt Carrol was there, heard the story, looked pleased, and said something to Mrs. March, which made her beam with satisfaction and watch Amy with a face full

of pride and anxiety. A week later Amy did get her reward, but poor Jo found it hard to be glad: A letter had come from Aunt Carrol.

Mrs. March's face lit up. "Aunt Carrol is going abroad next month, and wants—"

"Me to go with her!" burst in Jo.

"No, dear, not you. It's Amy. I'm afraid it's partly your own fault, dear. When Aunt spoke to me the other day, she said, 'I planned at first to ask Jo, but as "favors burden her" and she "hates French," I think I won't invite her. Amy is more docile, will make a good companion for Flo, and receive gratefully any help the trip may will give her.' "

There was not much time for preparation. Jo managed very well till the last flutter of blue ribbon vanished; then she retired to her attic and cried till she couldn't cry anymore. Amy was brave, too, till the steamer was about to sail. Then she

suddenly realized that a whole ocean would be between her and those who loved her best, and she clung to Laurie, saying with a sob, "Oh, take care of them for me, and if anything should happen . . ."

CHAPTER 22

Tender Troubles

"Jo, I'm anxious about Beth. I'm sure there is something on her mind, and I want you to find out what it is. She sits alone a good deal, and doesn't talk to her father as much as she used to. I found her crying over the babies the other day. When she sings, the songs are always sad ones, and now and then I see a look on her face that I don't understand."

Jo said, "I think she is growing up, Mother. Beth's eighteen, but we don't realize it, and we treat her like a child, forgetting she's a woman."

An incident gave Jo a clue to the mystery. One afternoon when she was writing, she kept her eye on her sister, who seemed unusually quiet. Beth was sitting at the window dejectedly when suddenly someone passed below, whistling like an operatic blackbird, and a voice called out, "All serene! Coming in tonight."

Beth started, leaned forward, smiled and nodded, watched the passerby till his quick tramp died away, then said softly as if to herself, "How strong and well and happy that dear boy looks."

"Hum!" said Jo, still intent upon her sister's face, for the bright color had faded as quickly as it had come, the smile vanished, and a tear lay shining on the window ledge.

"Beth loves Laurie! I never dreamed of such a thing," Jo said to her mother. "I want to go away somewhere this winter for a change. I feel restless and anxious."

"Where will you go?"

"To New York. Mrs. Kirke wrote to you for some respectable young person to teach her children, Tina and Kitty, and to sew. I think I should suit her if I tried."

The plan was talked over in a family council and agreed upon. When all was settled, Jo told Laurie, but to her surprise, he took it very quietly.

"One thing I leave in your special care," Jo said to Beth, the night before she left, "is my boy. Be very good to him, won't you?"

"I'll do my best, for your sake," promised Beth.

When Laurie said good-bye, he whispered, "It won't do a bit of good, Jo. My eye is on you, so mind what you do, or I'll come and bring you home."

CHAPTER 23

Jo's Journal

New York, November—

Dear Marmee and Beth, I've got heaps to tell. I saw a gentleman come along behind the little maid, and take the heavy hod of coal out of her hand, saying, with a kind nod and a foreign accent, "It goes better so. The little back is very young to haf such heaviness."

When I told this to Mrs. K., she simply laughed and said, "That must have been Professor Bhaer." He is from Berlin, very learned and good, but he is poor; he gives lessons to support himself and his two little orphan nephews.

Tuesday Eve—

Someone began to hum "Kennst Du Das Land," like a big bumblebee. I peeped in. Professor Bhaer was there. A regular German—rather stout, with brown hair, a bushy beard, good nose, the kindest eyes, and a splendid big voice. His clothes were rusty, his hands were large, and he had only beautiful teeth. I liked him.

Thursday—
Yesterday I was introduced to the professor. It seems as if I am doomed to see a good deal of him.

Saturday—
When I got back there, I saw Mr. Bhaer down on his hands and knees, with Tina on his back, Kitty leading him with a jump rope.

"Dis is mine effalunt!" added Tina, holding on by the professor's hair.

The "effalunt" sat up, and said soberly to me, I gif you my wort, if we make too large a

noise, you shall say Hush! to us, and we go more softly. I wish if Americans were as simple and natural as Germans, don't you?

Give heaps of love to everyone. From your faithful Jo.

CHAPTER 24

A Friend

Though very happy and very busy, Jo still found time to write. The dream of filling home with comforts, giving Beth everything she wanted, going abroad herself, and always having more than enough had been, for years, Jo's most cherished dream.

She took to writing sensation stories. And, the money was good. She saved most of what she earned. While she wrote, Jo was discovering a live hero. Mr. Bhaer had advised her to study simple, true, and lovely characters, wherever she found them, as good training for a writer. Jo took him at

his word, and studied him.

She began to see that character is a better possession than money, rank, intellect, or beauty, and to feel that if greatness is what a wise man had defined it to be, "truth, reverence, and good will," then her friend Friedrich Bhaer was not only good, but great.

And when she left to go home, she

invited him to visit.

Early as it was, he was at the station to see Jo off, and she began her journey with the pleasant memory of a familiar face smiling farewell, a bunch of violets to keep her company, and best of all, the happy thought, Well, the winter's gone, and I've written no books, earned no fortune, but I've made a friend worth having.

CHAPTER 25

Heartache

Laurie studied hard that year, and graduated with honors. They were all there, his grandfather, Mr. and Mrs. March, John and Meg, Jo and Beth, and all were proud of him. When he went home, Jo was there to meet him. But she was determined to keep her distance and not give him any encouragement. But he was as determined to speak.

"I've loved you ever since I've known you, Jo. I've tried to show it. Now I'm going to make you hear, and give me an answer, for I can't go on so any longer."

"You are a great deal too good for me, and I'm grateful. I am proud and fond of you. I don't know why I can't love you as you want me to. I've tried, but I can't," Jo told Laurie.

When Laurie came home, tired but calm, his grandfather was waiting. The old man said, "Take it like a man, and don't do anything rash. Why not go abroad, as you planned? I will go with you. It will do me good. I've friends in London and Paris, and should like to visit them. Meantime you can go to Italy, Germany, Switzerland, wherever you will."

Laurie sighed. "Just as you like, sir. It doesn't matter where I go or what I do."

That was Laurie's heartache. But Jo suffered differently.

When Jo came home that spring, Beth had changed. There was a strange, transparent look about it. Jo took Beth to the seashore, where the fresh sea breezes blew a little color into her pale cheeks.

One day Beth told her. Jo thought she was asleep and watched her, trying to see signs of hope in the faint color on Beth's cheeks. Beth looked at her to say, "Jo, dear, I'm glad you know it. I've tried to tell you, but I couldn't."

"Is this what made you so unhappy in the autumn, Beth?" asked Jo.

"Yes, I gave up hoping then, but I didn't like to own it. I tried to think it was a sick fancy, and would not let it trouble anyone. But when I saw you all so well and strong and full of happy plans, it was hard to feel that I could never be like you, and then I was miserable, Jo."

"Oh, Beth, and you didn't tell me, didn't let me comfort and help you?"

Beth could not explain the faith that gave her courage to give up life, and cheerfully wait for death. "You'll tell them this when we go home?"

"I think they will see it," sighed Jo.

She was right. There was no need of any words when they got home, for Father and Mother saw it clearly.

Laurie had left with his grandfather to go abroad after Jo's refusal.

At three o'clock in the afternoon, all the fashionable world at Nice was seen on the Promenade des Anglais. Haughty English,

lively French, sober Germans, handsome
Spaniards, ugly Russians, meek Jews, and
free-and-easy Americans all drove, sat, or
sauntered there.

Along this walk, on Christmas Day,
a tall young man walked slowly. He

looked like an Italian, was dressed like an Englishman, and had the independent air of an American—and many female eyes stared. Then he saw a young lady, blond, and dressed in blue.

"Oh, Laurie, is it really you?" cried Amy with joy.

"I promised to spend Christmas with you, and here I am."

There was something not quite right, Amy could sense. She watched him carefully, and felt strangely shy, for he was changed. He was more handsome than ever, but older and graver.

Laurie looked at her as she had looked at him. Always mature for her age, she had gained a certain confidence and polish.

CHAPTER 26

On the Shelf

Meg's maternal instinct was very strong, and she was entirely absorbed in her little children.

John missed the wifely attentions he was used to, but as he adored his babies, he made no complaint. But three months passed, and Meg looked worn and nervous, the babies absorbed every minute of her time, the house was neglected, and so was her husband.

He bore it very patiently for six months, and then looked for comfort elsewhere.

Little Women

Scott John's friend had married and Mrs. Scott was a lively, pretty, agreeable girl. So he went to their house more often than not.

And gradually, Meg began to miss John, and feel that she was not as attractive as before. When she complained to her mother, Marmee said, "You have only made the mistake that most young wives make—forgotten your duty to your husband in your love for your children. Don't neglect husband for children, don't shut him out of the nursery, but let him have more to do with the management of Demi. Then let Hannah come and help you. You need the exercise, Hannah would enjoy the rest, and John would find his wife again."

Meg thought it over, found it was a very good idea, and acted upon it. It took a little while for her to get it right, but when she really did it, John did not appear to object. The children thrived under the paternal rule, while Meg recovered her spirits and got wholesome exercise, a little pleasure, and much confidential conversation with her sensible husband. Home grew homelike again.

Meg learned that a woman's happiest kingdom is home, and her highest honor the art of ruling not as a queen, but as a wise wife and mother.

CHAPTER 27

Lazy Laurence

Laurie went to Nice, France, intending to stay a week, and remained a month. He was tired of wandering around. Amy's familiar presence added charm to foreign lands. But, to Amy, Laurie didn't seem as good a man as he was before. But the two never quarreled. Amy was too well-bred, and just now Laurie was too lazy.

"Laurie, when are you going to your grandfather's?" she asked.

"Very soon."

"You have said that a dozen times within the last three weeks. What would Jo say if she saw you now?" asked Amy, starting to draw Laurie as he lounged next to her.

"As usual, 'Go away, Teddy. I'm busy!'"

"I wish you'd do me the favor to rouse yourself a little," Amy said sharply. "I have a new name for you. It's Lazy Laurence."

"Why, if you please?"

"Because, with every chance for being good, useful, and happy, you are faulty, lazy, and miserable. I know I have no right to talk so to you, Laurie. But we are all so fond and proud of you, I couldn't bear to think they should be disappointed in you at home as I have been."

"You knew perfectly well I never cared for anyone but Jo," Laurie said.

"I did think so, but as they never said anything about it, and you went away, I supposed I was mistaken. And Jo wouldn't be kind to you? Why, I was sure she loved you dearly."

"She was kind, but not in the right way,

and it's lucky for her she didn't love me, if I'm the good-for-nothing fellow you think me. It's her fault, though, and you may tell her so."

"I was wrong, I didn't know. I'm very sorry I was so cross, but I can't help wishing you'd bear it better, Teddy, dear."

Laurie felt as if suddenly shaken out of a pensive dream and could not sleep again. He sat up and asked slowly, "Do you think Jo would despise me as you do?"

"Yes, if she saw you now. She hates lazy people."

Neither spoke for several minutes. Then Amy showed Laurie her sketch of him, saying, "How do you like that?"

He looked and then he smiled. It was very good—the long, lazy figure on the grass, with listless face, half-shut eyes, and one hand holding a cigar from which came a little wreath of smoke.

"As you are. This is as you were." Amy

showed him another sketch.

Only a rough sketch of Laurie taming a horse. Hat and coat were off, and every line of the active figure, face, and attitude was full of energy and meaning. Laurie said nothing, but as his eye went from one to the other, Amy saw him flush and fold his lips together.

"I found that sketch in my portfolio the other day, touched it up, and kept it to show you," she said.

"Much obliged. You've improved immensely since then." Laurie rose as he spoke, returned the pictures with a smile, and looked at his watch.

They laughed and chatted all the way home, but neither of them was happy. "Good-bye, dear," Laurie said, and with these words, he left her.

The next morning, Amy received a note from him: *Please say good-bye for me to your aunt. "Lazy Laurence" has gone to his grandpa.*

A pleasant winter to you.

"Good boy! I'm glad he's gone," said Amy. But she added with a sigh, "But how I shall miss him."

CHAPTER 28

The Valley of the Shadow

When the first feelings of sadness were over, the family accepted what was going to happen to Beth and tried to bear it cheerfully. They put aside their grief and tried to make that last year a happy one for her.

The nicest room in the house was Beth's, and had everything that she most loved—flowers, pictures, her piano, the little worktable, the cats, Father's best books, Mother's easy chair, Jo's desk, and Amy's finest sketches. And every day Meg brought her babies to visit. John quietly saved money

Little Women

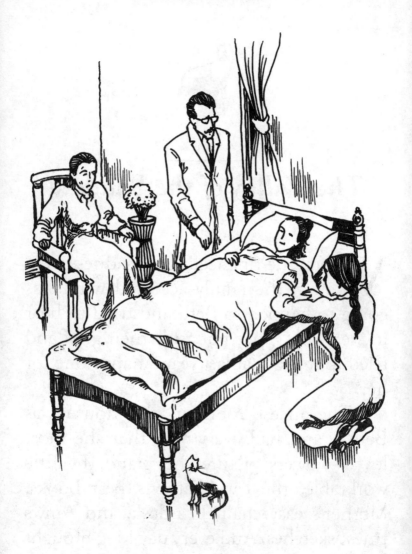

to buy her the fruit she loved and longed for. Old Hannah cooked for her every day, and from Amy came little gifts and cheerful letters.

Here sat Beth, tranquil and busy as ever. The first few months were very happy ones, and Beth often used to look around and say, "How beautiful this is!" as they all sat together in her sunny room, the babies kicking and crowing on the floor, mother and sisters working near, and father reading in his pleasant voice.

Soon Beth said the needle was "so heavy." Talking tired her, faces troubled her, the pain grew. As her body got weaker, Beth's soul grew stronger.

Jo stayed with her all the time, since Beth had said, "I feel stronger when you are here." Jo learned all about patience and charity, loyalty and duty. Often Jo found Beth reading her Bible, singing softly, and sometimes crying without any sound at all.

One night Beth found a little poem, in Jo's scribble. Poor Jo! She's fast asleep, so I won't wake her. She shows me all her things, and I don't think she'll mind if I look at this, thought Beth.

MY BETH

Sitting patient in the shadow
Till the blessed light shall come,
A serene and saintly presence
Sanctifies our troubled home.
Earthly joys and hopes and sorrows
Break like ripples on the strand
Of the deep and solemn river
Where her willing feet now stand.
. . .
Give me, for I need it sorely,
That courage, wise and sweet,
Which has made the path of duty
Green beneath your willing feet.
Give me that unselfish nature,

Little Women

That with charity devine
Can pardon wrong for love's dear sake
Meek heart, forgive me mine!

The poem brought Beth great comfort. As she sat with the paper in her hands, the charred log fell apart. Jo woke up, revived the blaze, and looked at her sister.

"Not asleep, but so happy. See, I found this and read it. I knew you wouldn't care. Have I been all that to you, Jo?" she asked.

"Oh—Beth, very much, very much!" Jo cried.

"Then I don't feel as if I've wasted my life. And now, when it's too late to begin even to do better, it's such a comfort to know that someone loves me so much, and feels as if I'd helped them. I shall be your Beth still, to love and help you more than ever. You must take my place, Jo, and be everything to Father and Mother when I'm gone."

"I'll try, Beth," Jo then promised.

So the spring days came and went, the earth got greener, and the birds came back in time to say good-bye to Beth. As she had hoped, the "tide went out easily," and in the dark hour before dawn, held in her mother's arms, she quietly died.

CHAPTER 29

Learning to Forget

Amy's lecture did Laurie good, though he did not admit it till long afterward. He went back to his grandfather's and was dutifully devoted to him. He decided to compose music, but kept getting distracted again and again by his thoughts of Jo and Amy. Laurie began to wish he had to work for his daily bread. To his great surprise he discovered it grew easier every day to forget his love for Jo. And he found himself thinking more about Amy instead.

Amy was having her own adventures. Fred Vaughn had asked her to marry him, and she, surprised at herself, said, "No, thank you." She wanted to be loved, not just to be a queen of society. And when she allowed herself to think about it, she found that she missed Laurie.

Amy grew a little pale and quiet that spring, lost much of her relish for society, and went out sketching alone a good deal. She sat for hours on the terrace at Valrosa, or sketched tall men with curly hair. The letter saying that Beth was dying never reached Amy, and when she finally read that her sister had died, it was too late to say good-bye to her, so everyone decided that Amy should stay in Europe.

Laurie came to see her very soon. She was sitting on a stone bench in a garden at the edge of the lake. Her head was on her hand, and she was thinking of Beth and wondering why Laurie did not come. She did not hear him cross the courtyard and walk toward her. He stood for a minute

looking at her, seeing what no one had ever seen before: the tender side of Amy's character. Everything about her suggested love and sorrow—the letters in her lap, the black ribbon in her hair, the pain and patience in her face, even the little ebony cross around her neck. She looked up and saw him and, dropping everything, she ran to him, saying with love and longing, "Oh, Laurie, Laurie, I knew you'd come to me!"

As he sat down beside her, Amy felt shy again. "I couldn't help it, I felt so lonely and sad, and was so very glad to see you. It was such a surprise to look up and find you," she said.

"I came the minute I heard. I wish I could say something to comfort you."

"You needn't say anything. This comforts me," she said softly. "Beth is happy now. You don't have to go right back, do you?"

Amy spoke and looked so like a homesick child that Laurie forgot he was shy, too. "Poor little soul, I'm going to take care of you so don't cry anymore, but come and walk with me," he said. After a while, they went back to the nearby hotel for dinner.

Laurie was always walking, riding, boating, or studying, while Amy admired everything he did and followed his example. The air did them both good, and so did the exercise. In spite of the sadness, it was a very happy time. There was no need for Laurie to tell Amy that he loved her— she knew it already. It all happened very easily and naturally.

One afternoon, the two were in a boat on the lake. Amy had been dabbling her hand in the water, and when she looked up, Laurie was leaning on the oars and watching her. She said, "You must be tired. Rest a little, and let me row."

Amy rowed well, and though she used both hands, and Laurie used only one, the boat went smoothly through the water.

"How well we pull together, don't we?" said Amy.

"So well that I wish we might always pull in the same boat. Will you, Amy?" he asked very tenderly.

"Yes, Laurie," she said in a very soft and low voice.

CHAPTER 30

All Alone

Jo found her promise very hard to keep. How could she "comfort Father and Mother" when her own heart ached?

"I can't do it. I wasn't meant for a life like this, and I shall break away and do something desperate if somebody doesn't come and help me," she said to herself.

But someone did come and help her: her mother. Jo's burden seemed easier to bear from the safe shelter of her mother's arms. And one day she went to her father's study and asked, "Father, talk to me as you did to Beth. I need it more than she did."

Then, sitting in Beth's little chair close beside him, Jo told him all her troubles. He gave her the help she needed, and both felt better. Jo took over Beth's duties of dusting and cleaning and humming songs as she worked. And everyone was happier.

And she found that the idea of marriage was not too bad, either. Meg had changed so much for the better, and Jo said to Meg when she came to visit one day with her children, "Marriage is an excellent thing, after all. I wonder if I should become as good as you, if I tried it."

"It's just what you need, Jo." Meg laughed, for she was glad to see a little of Jo's old spirit.

"Why don't you write again? That always used to make you happy," said her mother once, when Jo was hit by a wave of sadness.

"I've no heart to write, and if I had, nobody cares for my things."

"We do. Write something for us."

"Don't believe I can." But Jo got out her desk and began to overhaul her half-finished manuscripts. Jo never knew how it happened, but something got into one story that went straight to the hearts of those who read it. Her father sent it to one of the popular magazines, and to her utter surprise, it was not only paid for, but more asked for. Everyone liked it, friends and readers alike.

"I don't understand it. What can there be in a simple little story like that to make people praise it so?" she said.

"There is truth in it, Jo—that's the secret. You wrote with no thoughts of fame and money, and you put your heart in it."

So Jo wrote her little stories, and they were all published and praised.

When Amy and Laurie wrote about their engagement, Jo asked, "You like it, Mother?"

"Yes, I hoped it would be so, ever since Amy wrote that she had refused Fred."

"Truly, love does work miracles. How very happy they must be now!" Jo said, and smiled.

But Jo was restless. She went up to the garret and looked through her old books and papers. When she found a message written by the professor, she remembered him and his kindness and she sat down and cried.

CHAPTER 31

Surprises

Jo was alone, lying on the old sofa, looking at the fire, and thinking. It was her favorite way of spending the evening. No one disturbed her. She was twenty-five and feeling old and tired. "An old maid, that's what I'm to be," she said, and sighed.

Jo must have fallen asleep, for suddenly Laurie's ghost seemed to stand before her. She looked up, not really understanding, till he bent down and kissed her. She stood up, crying joyfully, "Oh, my Teddy!"

"Dear Jo, why, you are really glad to see me, then?"

"Glad! My blessed boy, words can't express my gladness. Where's Amy?"

"Your mother has got her down at Meg's. We stopped there, and there was no getting my wife out of their clutches."

"Your what?" cried Jo. "You've gone and got married!"

"Yes, please, but I never will again," he said, and he went down upon his knees, his hands together, and a face full of mischief, mirth, and triumph.

"Mercy on us. What dreadful thing will you do next?" Jo said, and laughed.

"How good it sounds to hear you say 'Teddy'! No one ever calls me that but you." And Laurie sat down.

"What does Amy call you?"

"My Lord. Don't I look like a married man and the head of a family?"

"Not a bit, and you never will."

"Now really, Jo, you ought to treat me with more respect," began Laurie.

"How can I, when the mere idea of you, married and settled, is so funny!" answered Jo.

"Well, I did it only to please Amy," began Laurie.

"Fib number one. And Amy did it to please you."

"It's all the same, you know, she and I being one. Grandpa wanted to come home. He went to please me, and I couldn't let him go alone, neither could I leave Amy. So I just settled the difficulty by saying, 'Let's be married, and then we can do as we like.'"

"When, where, how?" asked Jo.

"Six weeks ago, at the American consul's, in Paris, a very quiet wedding, for we didn't forget dear little Beth."

Jo said, "No, I had Father and Mother to help me, and the dear babies to comfort me, and the thought that you and Amy were safe and happy, to make the troubles here easier to bear. I am lonely, sometimes, but I dare say it's good for me, and—"

"You never shall be again," broke in Laurie, putting his arm about her.

Amy's voice was heard calling, "Where is she? Where's my dear old Jo?"

In trooped the whole family, and everyone was hugged and kissed all over again. Mr. Laurence was hale and hearty as ever. Jo thought, as she watched Laurie and Amy, I was right, and Laurie has found the beautiful, accomplished girl he needed. Mrs. March and her husband smiled and nodded at each other with happy faces. Amy's face showed a peaceful heart, her voice had a new tenderness in it, and the cool, prim carriage had changed to a gentle dignity.

"Love has done much for

our little girl," said her mother softly.

Jo felt very sad for a minute and decided, "I'll weep a little weep when I go to bed." Then, as she was going to join the others, there was a knock at the door.

She opened it, and there stood a

tall, bearded gentleman beaming at her from the darkness like a midnight sun. "Oh, Mr. Bhaer, I am so glad to see you!" cried Jo. "Come in."

Jo pulled him into the house and took his hat.

"You have been ill, my friend?"

As Jo hung up his coat, the light fell on her face, and he saw a change in it.

"Not ill, but tired and sorrowful. We have had trouble since I saw you last."

"Ah, yes, I know. My heart was sore for you when I heard that," he said, and shook her hand again, and Jo felt comforted.

"Father, Mother, this is my friend, Professor Bhaer," she said with so much pride that she might as well have blown a trumpet. Mr. Bhaer received a warm welcome upstairs.

Everyone greeted him kindly, for Jo's sake at first, but very soon they liked him for his own. If Jo had not been busy,

Laurie's behavior would have amused her. At first he stood back and frowned, faintly jealous, and then he got interested. Mr. Bhaer looked at Jo wistfully, but she kept her eyes on the little sock she was knitting and peeked at him every now and then.

CHAPTER 32

My Lord and Lady

Laurie said to his wife, "Mrs. Laurence, that man intends to marry our Jo!"

"I hope so, don't you, dear?" Amy was smiling. "Shall you care if Jo does marry Mr. Bhaer?"

"I assure you, I can dance at Jo's wedding with a heart as light as my heels. Do you doubt it, my darling?"

Amy looked up at him, and she was very satisfied.

"I wish we could do something for that capital old professor. Couldn't we invent a rich relation, who shall die in Germany,

and leave him a tidy fortune?" said Laurie.

"Jo would find us out and spoil it all. She is very proud of him, just as he is, and said yesterday that she thought poverty was a beautiful thing."

CHAPTER 33

Jo's World

Daisy and Demi were now almost four years old. And they were well on the way to being very spoiled by everyone. They were bright and happy. And they got along very well together. Daisy was Demi's slave and made friends with everyone, while Demi defended his sister from everybody else but ruled over her all the time.

Aunt Dodo, as Jo was called, was chief playmate and confidante of both children, and the trio turned the little house topsy-turvy. Aunt Amy was still only a name to them, and Aunt Beth soon faded into

memory. But when Mr. Bhaer came, Jo forgot her little friends. Demi soon found that Dodo liked to play with "the bear-man" better than she did him, but he didn't mind that much since his rival kept chocolate drops in his pocket. Daisy used his shoulder as her throne, and looked for the gifts he always brought them.

Mr. Bhaer was very correct. He always talked to Mr March. But Demi soon let the secret out. "Do great boys like great girls,

"Fessor?'"

Mr. Bhaer "couldn't tell a lie," so replied that they did sometimes. And that made Mr. March look at his daughter and think hard.

Jo and Mr. Bhaer were spending more time together, going for long walks and talking. And after they were done, Jo asked him home for coffee, "as Friedrich—I mean Mr. Bhaer—doesn't like tea."

By the second week, everyone knew perfectly well what was going on, but they never asked Jo about it. They all waited for her to speak to them, even Laurie, who was dying to tease his friend.

When the professor was absent for three days, Jo became quiet. "Disgusted, I dare say, and gone home as suddenly as he came. It's nothing to me, but I should think he would have come and bid us good-bye like a gentleman," she said to herself.

Still rather annoyed, she went out for a

walk and to do some shopping. And when it started raining, she found that a blue umbrella was being held over her head. She looked up and saw Mr. Bhaer looking down.

In a minute she found herself walking arm in arm with her professor, feeling as if the world was all right again. "We thought you had gone," said Jo hastily.

"Did you believe that I should go with no farewell to those who haf been so kind to me?" he asked.

Mr. Bhaer could read many languages, but he had not learned to read women yet. But he saw a small tear on Jo's cheek. Suddenly stooping down, he asked, "Heart's dearest, why do you cry?"

"Because you are going away."

"Jo, I haf nothing but much love to gif you. I came to see if you could care for it, and I waited to be sure that I was something more than a friend. Am I? Can you make a

little place in your heart for old Fritz?" he added, all in one breath.

"Oh, yes!" said Jo, and looked up at him with an expression that plainly showed how happy she would be to walk through life beside him.

Passersby probably thought them a pair of harmless lunatics, for they forgot to hail a bus, and strolled along. The professor looked as if he had conquered a beautiful kingdom, and Jo felt as if her place had always been there.

CHAPTER 34

Harvest Time

For a year, Jo and her professor worked and waited, hoped and loved, met occasionally, and wrote long letters to each other. In the second year, Aunt March died suddenly. And she left her big house to Jo.

Jo and Professor Bhaer decided that they would live there. And Jo said to Laurie, "I want to open a school for little lads—a good, happy, homelike school, with me to take care of them and Fritz to teach them. This isn't a new idea of mine. Before my Fritz came, I used to think how, when I'd made my fortune, and no one needed me at home, I'd hire a big house, and pick up some poor, forlorn little lads who hadn't any mothers, and take care of them. I told my plan to Fritz, and he said it was just what he would like, and agreed to try it when we got rich. Plumfield is just the place for boys, the house is big, and the furniture strong and plain. There's plenty of room, and splendid grounds outside."

Laurie asked, "But how you intend to support the place?"

"Of course I shall have rich pupils, also. Then, when I've got a start, I can take in a ragamuffin or two."

Things seemed to happen very fast. Almost before she knew where she was, Jo found herself married and settled at Plumfield. Then a family of six or seven boys sprung up, and flourished, poor boys as well as rich, all helped out by the clever Mr. Laurence.

Jo made queer mistakes, but the wise

professor always sorted things out. It wasn't a fashionable school, but it was just what Jo intended it to be: "a happy, homelike place for boys, who needed teaching, care, and kindness." And Jo was a very happy woman there, with her family, her boys, her Papa Bhaer, and her own two sons—Rob, named for Grandpa, and Teddy, a happy-go-lucky baby.

Seeing her happy family, Mrs. March stretched her arms as if to gather her children to herself and wished her girls a happiness that would last forever.

About the Author

American novelist Louisa May Alcott was born on November 29, 1832, into a poor family that believed in "plain living and high thinking." She was the second of four sisters.

Because of the family's poverty, she began work at an early age as an occasional teacher, seamstress, governess, and she was also a nurse for some time. She started writing under the pseudonym A.M. Barnard but tasted success in writing wholesome stories for children and young adults.

She is best known for the novel *Little Women*, a semi-autobiographical account of her childhood experiences with her sisters in Concord, Massachusetts. The second part to her successful novel is titled *Good Wives*. Other books by her are *Little Men* and *Jo's boys*.

Louisa died on March 6, 1888.